ROARASAURUS
THE ROARING SOARING DINOSAUR!

**Great-Aunt Rita
(and she really is GREAT)
with lots of help from Jake and
Elina Farber**

Illustrator: Mike Sofka

Fulton Books
Meadville, PA

Published by Fulton Books 2022

ISBN 979-8-88505-306-8 (paperback)
ISBN 978-1-63985-465-3 (hardcover)
ISBN 978-1-63985-464-6 (digital)

Printed in the United States of America

Dedication

To my great-nieces and great-nephews Sarah, Julia, Michael, Elina, and Jake, who also are really GREAT, and to whom I have told lots of tall tales.

Acknowledgements

Thanks to Susan Spitz, for her editorial expertise. Thanks to Marsha Cohen, Mary Clarke-Carrberry, Igor Elman, Lou Riceberg, and Liz Vargas for their helpful ideas and inspirations.

hat you are about to read is absolutely true—every single word. It may seem unbelievable, but it all really happened.

It was Jake's birthday, and Great-Aunt Rita wanted to get him something very special. When she went to the store, she saw many toys. But one toy, in particular, caught her eye. It was a big dinosaur—a *Tyrannosaurus Rex* (*T. Rex*). She said to herself, "My great-nephew loves dinosaurs and he even knows all of their names. I think he will love this present!"

5

When she took the dinosaur to the cash register, the man said, "What a fine toy. But do you know that this dinosaur is special?"

It can walk and talk. It can roam around your house and make dinosaur noises, while its eyes sparkle and its mouth glows.

So Great-Aunt Rita bought the toy for Jake. She knew he would have lots of fun with it.

When Jake got his present, he was so happy. His sister Elina watched while he ripped open the wrapping paper and took the dinosaur out of the box.

But to his great disappointment, when he started to play with it, it didn't walk or talk!

So Great-Aunt Rita read the instructions and found out that the toy needed batteries.

She put them in, and Elina pressed the ON button. Much to everyone's delight, the dinosaur started walking and talking.

The only problem was that it wasn't just walking and talking. It was running and roaring, turning the whole house topsy-turvy!

Jake and Elina were so scared they were shaking. They called out, "Please make it stop!"

Great-Aunt Rita hit the OFF button. But the dino just kept running and roaring!

Then, she even took the batteries out of the toy, but that dino still kept running and roaring!

Jake and Elina had to dodge the running dino and hold their ears to block out the roaring. It seemed like the more they screamed, the more the dino roared.

13

Jake and Elina suggested many names for that dinosaur, such as Rory, Rex-A-Roar, and Squawkasaurus.

But the name they liked the best was Roarasaurus because it seemed as if the dino was roaring and soaring throughout the room.

Great-Aunt Rita wrapped the running and roaring toy in blankets and put it on her back porch. That way, no one could see it running or hear it roaring.

But believe it or not,

Roarasaurus kept running and roaring on the porch for three days until Great-Aunt Rita finally brought it back to the store.

The very minute she walked into the store, the dinosaur stopped running and roaring.

The store clerk saw only a still, quiet dinosaur. But, he did believe that it had been running and roaring. So, the nice man allowed Great-Aunt Rita to return the dinosaur and gave her back her money.

When the holidays came, Jake's mother bought him a present she thought he would love. When he opened the present, it was the same dinosaur!

He screamed and ran away. He told his mother, "That dino has a mind of its own!" And Elina exclaimed, "Yes, that toy always makes a huge ruckus. It's a big troublemaker!"

Jake begged his mother to return it because he didn't want to see or hear any more running or roaring from Roarasaurus again.

His mother suggested, "Instead of returning it, why don't you try to tame it?"

"How do I do that?" Jake asked. His mother replied, "You make friends with it. Each of us, even a toy dinosaur, needs a friend. Spend time with it. Listen to it. Get to know it. Show it some good loving, and hug it a bunch."

Jake took his mother's advice. And then Roarasaurus didn't run or roar at all. It just walked and talked. It roamed around the house and made dinosaur noises, while its eyes sparkled and its mouth glowed! It did just what it was supposed to do.

Jake smiled at his mother and said, "I think I will keep this dinosaur after all. I know we can have lots of fun together. And, it feels great to have a new friend. I think Roarasaurus is the best toy a child could ever have!"

AGAIN, READ IT AGAIN, AGAIN

About the Author

Great-Aunt Rita (and she really is GREAT), aka Rita Berman, MD, MPH, spent many years as a physician. She now spends lots of time with her great-nephew Jake and her great-niece Elina (and they really are GREAT too). She got to be a "grandma" without having kids, so much so, that Jake called her "Grandma-Aunt Rita".

Based on a true story, *Roarasaurus The Roaring Soaring Dinosaur!* was written when Jake was five and Elina was eight years old. This is their first published book.

CPSIA information can be obtained
at www.ICGtesting.com
Printed in the USA
BVHW022122010922
646108BV00002B/18